Mother's Manners

Chita Johnson

Order this book online at www.trafford.com
or email orders@trafford.com

Most Trafford titles are also available at major online book retailers.

Printed in the United States of America.

ISBN: 978-1-4669-4733-7 (sc)
ISBN: 978-1-4669-4732-0 (e)

Trafford rev. 10/24/2012

 www.trafford.com

North America & international
toll-free: 1 888 232 4444 (USA & Canada)
phone: 250 383 6864 ♦ fax: 812 355 4082

I am dedicating this book to my mother, who loved me enough to teach me nice manners. Not just once in a while, but daily.

I am dedicating this book to my father, who taught me nice manners by example. I will always remember how he supported my mother by agreeing with her. When my father passed away on October 15, 2006, most of the people who visited me at his memorial service said, "Your father was the perfect gentleman." I never knew people thought that about my father until he died.

I am dedicating this book to every boy who has won "The Perfect Gentleman" award at Alta Loma Junior High School which is awarded annually in honor of my father.

I am dedicating this book to the National Charity League of Alta Loma, CA. I have thoroughly enjoyed being your manners/modelette instructor for the past ten years. Thank you for your kind hearts and delightful attitudes.

I am dedicating this book to my husband, Paul, and our beautiful children, Adam and Chita Katherine.

ABOUT THE AUTHOR

Chita Beasley Bacon Johnson delights in sharing how being born and raised in the South by caring parents continually focused on teaching her nice manners. The only way to truly acquire proper manners and treat others with respect is to walk it and talk it on a daily basis. Experience is the key to a greater understanding of anything. I was fortunate to have been elected Cleveland's Teen Board representative in high school my sophomore year. This honor gave me a reason to work at becoming graceful, walk with poise, and exemplify proper social manners. While representing Cleveland, TN, at parties and functions in a larger city, Knoxville, TN, I was learning how being "ladylike" was impressive in social situations. I was later elected "Most Popular" of my senior class. When I look back, that was solely based on being friendly and courteous to my peers on a daily basis. Even though I didn't win Cleveland's Junior Miss Pageant, I enjoyed walking and talking with eloquence during training sessions to compete in this event for an extended period of time. I later became a debutante my sophomore year of college. Both experiences, Teen Board Representative and Debutante required a formal white gown, elbow length white gloves and a formal presentation. I attended around thirty parties in the homes of the most prominent people of Cleveland the year I was a debutante. It was exciting for me to learn how to dress properly for a party and socialize in an appropriate fashion.

After graduating from the University of Tennessee at Knoxville in Physical Education, I married and had two children. When Chita Katherine was four and Adam was eight we moved to Alta Loma, California so my husband could continue working in the building industry. I transferred as a provisional into the Junior League of Riverside, in which I was able to meet some of the nicest, most accomplished women in the city. Voluntary community service work and fund raising parties were emphasized in order to help others and serve the community as needed. I was being formally trained socially while practicing how to host parties. We also trained our daughters, called Tic Tockers, to help us host holiday parties. This created a fun way to raise girls in style, with grace, through party etiquette. I often referred to books written by manners experts such as Emily Post, Amy Vanderbilt, and Hermine Hartley in case I needed advice pertaining to a specific social situation.

In 1994 I was featured as the Cover Girl for the Inland Empire Magazine. It was a thrill to be the fifth Cover Girl winner at 38 years old! The contest was based off of three photos and an interview. I am certain to this day that my interviewing skills won it for me. I used the same mannerisms Mother had taught me as a little girl which clearly worked!

I later attained my masters in Curriculum and Instruction from Chapman University. While teaching physical education at a junior high school I began to realize the need to teach children the correct way to act in social situations. It was sad for me to witness the lack of respect and tidiness missing in our girl's locker room, lunch area, and campus area throughout the day. During this same time I was the modeling and manners instructor locally for John Robert Powers and National Charity League. For the past twenty years I have taught manners, modeling, and etiquette in local modeling agencies and privately in my home upon request.

There's one thing I know for sure and that is every good mother and father hope their children know how to react and behave appropriately in social situations. Some parents aren't quite sure how to teach their children how to act in a proper fashion socially or even sure what nice manners really are. (I found this out from teaching "dining do's and don'ts" around my dining room table for the past twenty years.) Some people feel having proper table manners and setting a table properly is becoming a lost art. For this reason alone I have written "Mothers Manners". I am merely passing on to the world the manners I was taught as a child and have practiced my entire life.

BENEFITS OF HAVING NICE MANNERS

I almost named this book "Chita's Choice" because throughout my life experiences I simply chose to practice the manners my parents taught me. It was my choice to apply and practice their instruction, and it will be your choice too after reading this book. I recognized in elementary school that being friendly, respectful, and loving allowed me to make friends easily, socially be more poised and polished, act more ladylike, raise my confidence and self-esteem, please my parents and teachers, while helping me relax in social situations.

Later in life, as a mother, I felt smart being able to teach my children the rights and wrongs, the do's and don'ts pertaining to social situations on a daily basis. Kindness, helping others, a big smile, and proper up-bringing has helped my children thrive in this over competitive world in which we live. A happy disposition helped them stand out in a crowd.

My decision to practice and exercise "Mothers Mannes" has created a passion for manners and proper etiquette in my heart forever. My wish is that it does the same thing for you.

Just last week I was working in Los Angeles as a print model in a furniture store for a man and his production company to promote a product he invented. All of the pictures were taken of me while I was seated at a dining room table set up by a group of professional men in a production crew for fine dining. As I sat there preparing to smile for the camera, I noticed the silverware was set up backwards for a proper place setting. (In this case, the forks were on the right side of the dinner plate instead of the left side.) In my mind, this mattered for the sale of the product to be successful. In my quiet, most polite voice, I asked the product manager and director if they had noticed the silverware wasn't set up correctly. They both admitted neither one had noticed it. They immediately changed it and thanked me for helping them correct the situation. I honestly couldn't believe a bunch of professional people did not know how to set a table properly for fine dining. I feel thankful for this knowledge. After all, my passion for setting a table properly for dining goes back to what my mother first taught me.

This story "Mothers Manners" is about how I acquired nice manners from my parents, especially my mother. These are the same manners I have taught my children and students. This story depicts the value and importance of acquiring social etiquette through experience and practice on a daily basis. After you read this story you will hopefully want to acquire nice manners so you can become a role model in order to pass them on to others, especially your children.

Once upon a time there was a little girl named Chita Beasley Bacon. I was five years old and felt excited about moving into a newly built house on Joy Street in Cleveland, Tennessee. My parents loved me very much and proved it on a daily basis by teaching me nice manners. They knew that proper social skills would help me be kinder and a more likable person socially.

My mother hosted a birthday party for me when I was five years old. This party was fun for me because there was a cake, balloons, and a lot of gifts from my girlfriends. We all dressed up on a hot September day to look our best and celebrate my birthday. I was taught to say "thank you" at a very early age. I thanked the girls for the gifts they brought me whether I liked the gift or not. I also thanked the girls for coming. Whenever you thank someone for something, it teaches you to be more appreciative. My mother thought it was rude when people would mumble and look away when they were talking to someone. So I practiced looking at my friends in the eye when I talked to them. I practiced saying, "You're welcome" when my friends thanked me for something. Being appreciative and making friends with people who were giving and kind created a peaceful environment. A peaceful environment makes everyone feel loved and secure. Don't let a "thank you" go unsaid!

After my birthday party was over, I thanked my mother for giving me such a fun party. People want to do more nice things for you when you appreciate them and thank them. Children often act nicer and feel better about themselves when they dress up a little bit. It is better to over-dress for a friend's party than to be under-dressed. It shows respect for your friend and the occasion when you look your best. Your friend is hoping you will look and dress appropriately, as that makes them proud to be your friend.

My father was quiet and soft spoken around the house most of the time. He role modeled manners in a gentleman's way. He was extremely supportive of my mother verbally teaching me how to look people in the eye while talking to them. I enjoyed listening to mother, because I knew she was making me more personable.

The quickest way to allow an adult to know a child is respectful is to answer with "yes sir" or "yes ma'am". I was taught to never say "nope" or shake my head no to an adult to answer them. It's polite to speak up. "No sir" or "No ma'am" immediately let the adult know the parents had taught the children to respect adults. When people answer with one word it often comes across harsh or disrespectful. The more you talk, the more friendly you appear to be. The more conversation you have with someone, the bigger your personality seems to be. People love someone who responds and is easy to talk to.

Visiting friends and family as a child gave me a chance to practice having perfect posture by sitting and standing up straight. Perfect posture is more attractive than slumping. Standing up straight is a good exercise for your back and it helps your vertebrae to grow straight. People with perfect posture are more impressive to look at than people who slump or slouch. One of the first things you often notice about a person is their posture. Good or bad posture will leave a lasting impression.

I was elected Cleveland's Teen Board Representative when I was in high school. This meant I would represent the city of Cleveland, TN socially in Knoxville, TN at a brunch, a luncheon and dinner party/presentation. Each city had a representative and I was excited about the opportunity to meet new people, display proper table manners, and act poised at the presentation. I was able to invite ten of my best friends and their dates. We had parties and get-togethers to plan for the presentation. It was a formal affair for teenagers. It was important to dress appropriately for the parties and presentation.

This picture was taken at my neighbor's house and put in the local newspaper in order to announce the 1972 Cleveland Teen Board Representative.

My friends and I are having a few home parties in preparation for the teen board presentation.

BASIC WARDROBE GUIDELINES

Sportswear/Ballgame attire—jeans, khakis, warm-ups, sweat tops, work-out clothes, jerseys, tennis shoes, flip-flops, and shirts

Beachwear—short shorts, short dresses, sun dresses and skirts, casual pants, bathing suits, cover-ups, skimpy clothing, flip-flops, sandals, and tennis shoes

Casual—jeans, khakis, Capri, cargo, shirts, blouses, loafers, tennis shoes, simple basic dresses, skirts and pant outfits . . . . maybe tee shirts and flip-flops (depends on the location)

Buisness/Professional/Upscale Casual—suits, pant suits, professional looking clothes, church clothes, button-down shirts, blouses, pumps and closed toe shoes, keep the jewelry minimum and classy (pearls, gold or silver hoops that are no larger than a quarter) dress shoe for men, ties always look classy worn with a man's suit or sport coat

Absolutely NO jeans, tee shirts, sleeveless shirts, dirty shoes, tennis shoes, flip-flops, cargo pants, tops that show cleavage, not too clingy, cheap jewelry, sagging or bagging pants, too tight is tacky, shirt-tails hanging out is sloppy not cool

Semi-formal or After Five—dressy dresses and skirts (thigh high to calf length), cocktail clothes, sequins are appropriate, blingy jewelry is fine, suit and tie for men, dressy shoes, evening shoes

Formal or Black Tie—evening gowns (floor length or ankle length), dressy cocktail clothes, satin or silk pant outfit, dressy evening separates, sequins are appropriate, blingy jewelry is fine, tux or black suit for the men

Mother often took me with her when she would visit her friends. I learned to address adults respectfully. This meant calling them Mister and Mrs. (last name). Only adults can speak to adults by their first name, unless the adult advises them to do so.

When Mother and I visited friends and family, they often served us drinks and desserts. It's polite to offer a guest a drink or something to eat while they're visiting. Mother always said to say "Yes please", or "No thank you" when food was offered. It was considered rude and disrespectful to answer with one word since it was short and showed less personality. "Yeah", "nope", or merely shaking nodding your head were unacceptable answers. With practice I enjoyed learning how to talk to a variety of people in social situations with confidence. Whenever I was asked a question such as, "Would you care for a glass of lemonade Chita?" I was taught to answer, "Yes, I would love a glass of lemonade and thank you so much". Never answer a question with "whatever". One word answers don't show much personality or allow you to seem very friendly. Let's say I decided to answer their question with "no". I could answer by saying, "No, thank you, I don't care for a glass of lemonade, but I would love a glass of water". In this way I am able to act receptive and be polite at the same time without having to accept the lemonade.

My one-on-one time with Mother allowed me to learn privately how to treat other people in a polite way. Mother was kind to reprimand me in private if I had acted inappropriately. Occasionally, I was given a gift or trinket for stopping by. I was taught to say "thank you" and act appreciative whether I liked it or not. Being appreciative and thankful is a Godly way to act.

One of the most important things I learned to do when I was with a friend was to listen to them while they were talking. I tried to give them my undivided attention so they would feel my interest in them. I always appreciated it when people did that to me when I was talking. I grew to realize the people who were interested in me, and listened to me, were valuable friends. Having good listening skills will cause people to like you as you develop their friendship.

C onversation at the dinner table is important. Meals are a fun time to share your life with your family and friends. It's thoughtful not to talk too loud or be rude to others while they are talking. Imagine your words or conversation on a string while you are sitting at the table talking to others. "Strings" of conversation should never intersect. One person should not talk through another person. Everyone should listen to one person talk at a time in a social gathering with eight or less. This allows the conversation to stay on the quieter side and not get too loud. A person should never cut another person's story off with a new conversation while they're talking. It's rude! Be patient for your turn. Always allow each person to finish their story before you start a new one. Never say to a person, "Give me the two minute version of your story". This makes the person telling the story feel unimportant and less worthy than the other people at the table, because their time for talking has now been limited compared to the other people talking. That's a rude statement! Think about who you're going to sit by at dinner, because that's probably who you're going to talk to the most. You may talk to anyone at the table as long as your "strings" of conversation don't intersect. This particular etiquette also refers to standing in a group setting as well.

One of my favorite ways my parents taught my brother and I nice manners was to put a quarter above the door sill when we gathered at the kitchen table for dinner. They didn't do it every meal, but occasionally. Then mother would say, "O.K. Paul and Chita, whoever has the best table manners tonight, during dinner gets the quarter over the door sill". (I understand times have changed. You parents might have to give your children a $1.00 or whatever you think is a reasonable incentive for your child to practice proper table manners.) Believe it or not, the quarter was good enough for my brother and I. We waited for Mother to sit down so we could begin eating, bless the food, sit up straight, unfold our napkin in our laps, keep our elbows off the table the entire meal, chew with our mouths closed, chew slowly, not talk with food in our mouths, talk about things that are going on in our lives to one another so we actually enjoyed some family time together, use our flatware the American style, never let the flatware go back to the table after it had been used in any way during the meal, put our fork and knife on our dinner plate in a parallel position which indicated we were finished eating, wait patiently for each member of the family to finish before excusing ourselves from the table and last but not least . . . . remember to thank Mother for cooking or preparing such a delicious dinner! Even if it wasn't our favorite food, we were taught to be thankful. Mother believed practicing anything correctly helped you to get better at it.

If a phone rang during the meal, we first excused ourselves, then answered the phone and told the caller we would call them back in thirty minutes or so after we finished eating. It's not polite to take a call and talk for a while during a meal time with your family. It's rude to your family!

These were the basic rules my parents taught my brother and I to practice during meal times. I still live by them today. Hopefully, you won't make the incentive too expensive so the one who loses isn't sad about not winning the prize. A quarter was perfect for us, because no matter who won, the other one usually thought "good for you". It wasn't a great loss not to win the quarter, but it was always fun to win.

I was raised in a Christian home, so it was very important to bless the food we ate before each meal. One of my favorite blessings is:

Dear Heavenly Father,

Bless this food to the nourishment of our bodies,

And our bodies are for your service,

In Jesus name we pray,

Amen.

DINING DO'S AND DON'TS

Remember to:

1. Sit in the middle of the chair without using the back of the chair
2. Sit with perfect posture
3. Pull the chair forward under the table until your chin lines up with the edge of the table
4. Place your napkin which is on your left, in your lap unfolded
5. Be sure to bless the food
6. It is important to maintain perfect posture during the course of the meal. Each person should slightly lean forward to eat and slightly lean backward when people on either side of you want to talk to each other. Leaning back in your chair is a polite way of letting your friends see each other while they are talking to each other.
7. Allow the hostess to cue you when to eat by letting them take the first bite.
8. Mother always said, "Use your silverware from the outside in." This simply means to pick up the silverware on the far left and far right of the plate according to what is being served during the meal. For example, if salad is your first food served, then use your salad fork. Your salad fork is located on the far left of the salad plate. You may or may not need to use your knife to cut with.
9. Leave your silverware on the plate once it's been used (silverware is not allowed back on the table after it's been used)
10. Leave the salad fork and knife resting in a parallel position on the salad plate until the plate is removed from the table. The blade of the knife should be facing you.
11. Now serve the entrée on the dinner plate—once again, use the silverware on the outside left, which is the dinner fork and you may possibly have to ask for another dinner knife. I often keep my salad knife by placing the knife on my bread and butter plate in order to use the same knife for dinner. Then the salad

fork is the only utensil carried away with the salad plate. The dessert is served last and the only silverware left is the spoon, which is located on the right side of the dinner-plate. Sometimes a spoon and fork is placed above the dinner plate. Whichever one you choose to eat dessert with is okay!

12. At the end of the meal place your napkin to the left of your dinner plate in a fairly neat position—never on top of the dinner plate. Try to keep the area you ate in as neat and clean as possible.

13. Be patient and wait for others to finish eating

14. Excuse yourself to others before you leave the table.

15. Thank the cook or hostess for preparing the meal.

16. Keep your mouth closed while you are eating and drinking.

17. Wipe your mouth occasionally with a napkin.

18. Talk softly to your friend and never yell to someone across the room.

19. Don't point at people or things.

20. Don't whisper in front of other people—don't tell secrets.

21. Don't put your feet on furniture in any way.

22. Stand unless you are asked to sit down.

23. Try to meet and talk a little to everyone so you don't consume one person's time the entire evening. Introduce yourself to people you don't know, and try to enjoy getting to know them. Humble yourself.

24. Take a hostess gift to show appreciation for the invitation (usually under $10.00). It's the thought that counts! A small bouquet of flowers is appropriate. Even one beautiful flower in a small vase is kind.

25. If someone other than your date asks you to dance, be gracious, have fun, and go with it. Hopefully, your date is understanding and should respond by asking their date to dance. You might rather take advantage of that time to mingle and get to know other people, get something to eat, or just relax and take a break from dancing and talking. Keep in mind the purpose of going to a party is to have fun!

The proper way to use the fork and knife are pictured above. This is the American style of using a fork and knife. The fork is held in the left hand to secure food being cut with a knife held in the right hand. The knife is then placed across the plate and the fork is transferred to the right hand.

The European or Continental style of eating is when the fork remains throughout the meal in the left hand, while the knife is in the right hand.

When I was in third grade I learned how to set a table properly. Knowing how to set the table helped me practice using the silverware correctly during the meal.

When a table is set properly, it becomes a road map to what's being served and when. Remember to pick up your silverware in order, working from the outside in. Please remember the limit rule; if more than three of any utensil is needed, it will come with the course. Don't forget to hold your goblet by the body of the glass, not the stem.

A FORMAL PLACE SETTING

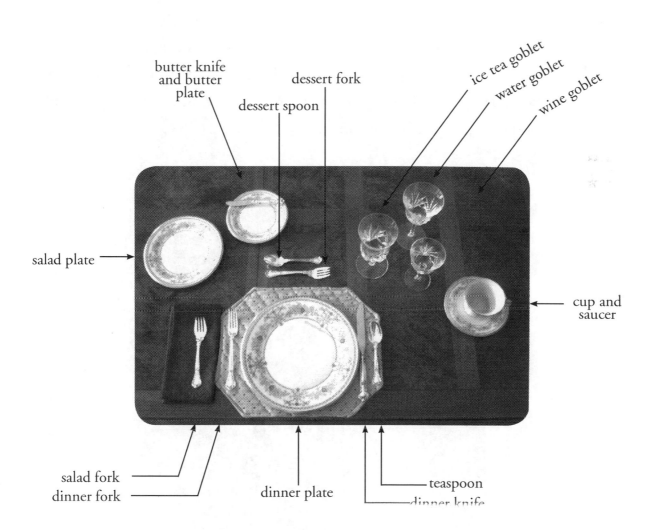

butter knife
and butter
plate

dessert spoon

dessert fork

ice tea goblet

water goblet

wine goblet

salad plate

cup and
saucer

salad fork
dinner fork

dinner plate

teaspoon

dinner knife

I was a debutante my sophomore year in college. During this time, "the women" of Cleveland taught the debutantes how to dress appropriately for each occasion and party. We also observed etiquette pertaining to socializing, dining, drinking, dancing, gift-giving, and making new friends. Here are some quick observations attending parties in general:

Chita Bacon and Paul Johnson

1. Always introduce your date as well as yourself to everyone you encounter at the party

2. Always introduce yourself and your date to the host and hostess right away when you get to the party

3. When you talk about yourself or others, say kind, positive things

4. Be complementary in a sincere way about anything

5. Always say the name of the oldest person first when you are making formal introductions. For example, "Mother, Daddy, this is Paul. He's my date to the deb party tonight. Paul, these are my parents, Mr. and Mrs. Bacon." When women and men are present, introduce the women first.

Social introductions were mandatory at the debutante parties. It was the only way for everyone to get to know one another. Sweet, honest social introductions make people feel loved. It is important for the hostess to introduce as many people as she possibly can at a party, standing at a gathering, or an informal one-on-one time with a friend. Social introductions allow people to feel comfortable instead of feeling awkward and uncomfortable. A proper introduction allows people to get to know one another and have more fun at the party.

Cleveland Daily Banner—Tuesday, September 17, 1974

DEB LUNCHEON—Mrs. W.K. Fillauer and daughter, Mrs. Jeff McKinney, were hostesses Saturday for a noon luncheon honoring Miss Chita Bacon, one of the 1974 Cotillion Holly Ball Debutantes. From left: Mrs. Paul Bacon, mother of the honored deb; Miss Bacon; Mrs. Fillauer and Mrs. McKinney. Miss Bacon will be among the debutantes in the 1974 Holly Ball scheduled in December at Cleveland Country Club.

HOSTESSING A PARTY

Having a party is fun, but it requires a lot of work. Setting up for the party is important, but what people usually remember about the party is how they were treated by others. When people are treated well by other people, you can usually count on them having a good time. If you host the party, it is your responsibility to make sure all of the people get introduced to each other and inter-mix. The hostess or host should spend most of their evening talking to all of their guests. The host needs to make sure the guests feel at home in their house by continually serving drinks, offering food, offering guidance to restrooms, and discussing the house in a way that is interesting to others. Always allow people to sit down so they can relax and feel at home. If you are hosting try not to spend the whole evening with one person. Talk to one person for a while, and then mention you don't want to consume their whole evening. It's an easy way to move on and visit with the next person. Try to make sure no one is alone without someone to talk to. Remember to thank your guests for coming, and they should thank you for having them. If you are a guest, it's polite to take a small gift to show your appreciation for being invited to the party.

The most important thing to remember when you receive an invitation is to RSVP. It means "respond if you please". And what that really means is to be thoughtful and responsible enough to call and let the hostess know if you're coming to their party or not. Sometimes an invitation will say, "regrets only". This means to call the hostess if you cannot attend the party. It is extremely rude not to respond accordingly. People hosting parties are giving their time, energy, and money on other people's behalf. The least people can do is respond to the hostess so they will know how many people are coming. This allows the hostess to know how much food, seating, space, drinks, etc., to provide for the occasion. This is especially true for weddings and receptions. Nothing is worse when you are giving a party than trying to imagine how many people are coming.

Whatever time the party starts, you should try to be there no later than fifteen minutes of that time. If you can't make it when the invitation requests, call the hostess and tell them why you will be coming late. This is a good time to remember the golden rule: "Do unto others as you would have them do unto you."

A fter graduating from the University of Tennessee at Knoxville, I married Paul Johnson. Many parties were given in our honor. The hostess of each event talked and helped everyone to feel comfortable and have fun!

4—Cleveland Daily Banner—Sunday, September 11, 1977

Parties Honor Couple

Mr. and Mrs. Paul Johnson, who were married recently, were complimented prior to their marriage, with several parties and courtesies. The bride is the former Chita Bacon.

The couple was honored with an old Southern Plantation Dinner Party held at the S.J. Sullivan home on North Ocoee Street. Hostesses for the occasion were Emma Jane Sullivan, Suzanne Appling, Debbie Forsten, Melanie Howle, Rita McKinney and Mary Belle Arnett.

Mrs. John L. Tye III was hostess for a luncheon recently at the Cleveland Country Club.

Mrs. William F. Johnson III was hostess for a tea honoring the bride. The tea was held at the Johnson home on Springhill Drive with Mmes. Tom Johnson and Robert Johnson as co-hostesses.

Miss Melanie Howle hosted a luau at the Loyd Howle home on Peerless Road. Mrs. Charles Anderson was co-hostess for the event.

A luncheon and shower was held at the W.K. Fillauer home. Hostesses were: Mrs. William Fillauer, Mrs. Jeff McKinney, Mrs. John Jaggers, Mrs. William Schultz and Mrs. Robert Taylor.

Mmes. Nelom Jackson, Tom Peden and Jim Reynolds were hostesses for a luncheon held at Cleveland Country Club.

A spinster dinner was hosted at the James Chase home. Mrs. James Chase and Mrs. Dean Chase III were hostesses for the occasion.

REHEARSAL DINNER—Mr. and Mrs. Paul Johnson, who were married this weekend, were complimented at a rehearsal dinner prior to their Sunday afternoon marriage. The bride is the former Chita Bacon. From left: Mrs. Robert Boonstra, grandmother of the bridegroom; Mrs. William F. Johnson, mother of the bridegroom; the newlyweds; Mrs. Paul Bacon and Mr. Bacon, parents of the bride.

Mrs. William A. Jones and daughters Amy and Ann were hostesses for the bridesmaids luncheon held at the Jones home on 21st St. NW.

Mrs. William F. Johnson, mother of the bridegroom, hosted the rehearsal dinner prior to the wedding. The occasion was held at the Ramada Inn.

The couple was wed Sunday at the Broad Street United Methodist Church.

It was important to take time out and let everyone introduce themselves and tell a few things about themselves while mingling at the party.

BACON—JOHNSON

Bacon - Johnson

CLEVELAND, Tenn., — Mr. and Mrs. Paul H. Bacon announce the engagement of their daughter, Miss Chita Beasley Bacon, to Paul Douglas Johnson, son of Mrs. William F. Johnson and the late Mr. Johnson.

The wedding is planned to take place on Sunday, September 4, at Broad Street United Methodist Church, where both are members.

The bride-elect is the granddaughter of Mrs. Oscar N. Beasley, the late Mr. Beasley of Elkton, Mrs. Ben H. Bacon and the late Mr. Bacon.

Miss Bacon received a B.S. degree in education from the University of Tennessee at Knoxville where she was a member of the UTK Women's Chorale and was ATO Sweetheart of 1976. She was a Cleveland Teen Board presentee in 1972 and is a member of the Cleveland-Athens Cotillion. She was presented at the 1974 Holly Ball.

(Stanfield)

(Fiancee of Paul D. Johnso|

Our local newspaper printed my engagement announcement.

BRIDESMAIDS LUNCHEON—Mrs. Paul Johnson, the former Chita Bacon, was guest of honor during a bridesmaids luncheon held at the William A. Jones residence. Mrs. Johnson (center) is flanked by Misses Amy and Ann Jones, hostesses for the occassion.

It's important to take pictures at your parties, so you can have wonderful memories of the event as time goes by.

PARTY—Mrs. Paul Johnson, the Chita Bacon, was guest of honor at a party held recently at the Jim Chase om left: Mrs. William F. Johnson, | mother of the bridegroom; Mrs. Jim Chase; Mrs. Paul Bacon, mother of the bride; the bride. and Mrs. Dean Chase, hostess.

Stanfiel

BRIDAL LUNCHEON—Misses Debra Miller and Chita Bacon, future brides, were honored recently with a luncheon given by Mrs. John Tye II. Miss Miller is the prospective bride of Bart | Carter and Miss Bacon is engaged to Johnson. From left are Mrs. H.B. Carter Fred Miller, Jr., Miss Miller, Miss Bacon Paul Bacon, Mrs. W.F. Johnson, and Mrs

A wedding shower at the home of Francis Fillauer

Any time you host a party for someone, you are honoring them and showing a lot of love! You can say "gifts" or "no gifts" on the invitation.

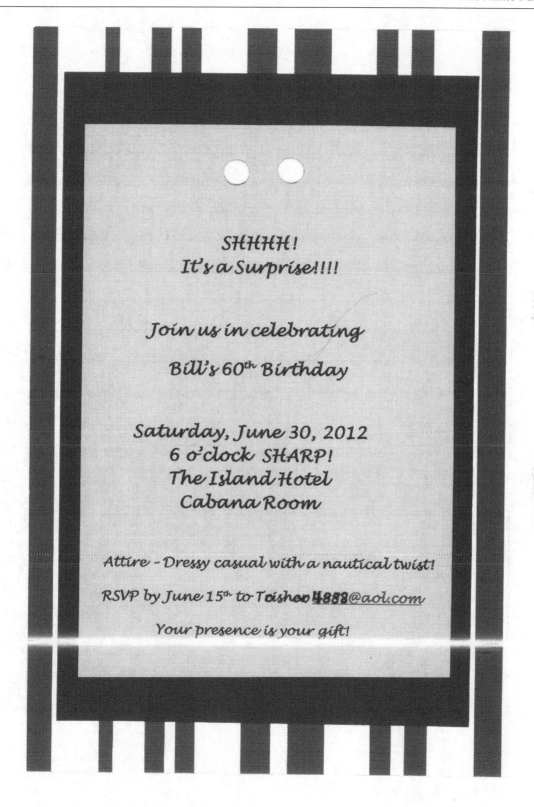

SHHHH!
It's a Surprise!!!!

Join us in celebrating

Bill's 60th Birthday

Saturday, June 30, 2012
6 o'clock SHARP!
The Island Hotel
Cabana Room

Attire – Dressy casual with a nautical twist!

RSVP by June 15th to Toishoo4888@aol.com

Your presence is your gift!

This invitation is the perfect example of giving your friends all the details of the party. Now they know what to wear, what to bring, and how to act when they get to the party. "Quiet" at first because it's clearly a surprise!

My husband and I moved our children to Alta Loma, California in 1988 due to job related reasons. On my return visit to Tennessee, Mother hosted a summer luncheon with some friends to welcome me home. That party made me feel missed and loved. Having a gathering or party to honor someone shows a lot of kindness on your part and love toward the other person.

After I married and had children, I was asked to join Junior League. This international association of women are committed to promoting voluntarism, developing the potential of women and improving communities through the effective action and leadership of trained volunteers. Its purpose is exclusively educational and charitable. Besides enjoying all the wonderful people affiliated with Junior League, I have a lot of fun attending their eloquent parties.

Once again, my mother's manners helped pave my way. After you learn to speak properly to others, you won't mind being around large groups of people in fun, social settings. You won't feel intimidated to meet new people and make new friends. It will become a natural act to look people in the eye and speak clearly to them.

When you join an organization you are given an opportunity to practice getting along with a variety of people. It's your responsibility to get to know them. It's impolite to be part of an organization and never talk to the people.

After teaching physical education for seventeen years at a public junior high school, I saw how rude and hurtful it is to the students when they make fun of each other. Slander and name calling are two of their favorite ways to communicate. Kind behavior toward one another is quite the challenge in such an extremely competitive environment. I witness broken hearts and hurt feelings on a daily basis among my students. I counsel an endless number of students on how to treat each other with respect. I often teach fifty boys and girls every fifty minutes, Monday through Friday, five periods a day. There are around 150 girls in my locker room every fifty minutes dressing out for physical education. I am trying to incorporate as much kindness and etiquette as I possibly can into my team sports and fitness program. After seventeen years of teaching, I have found students love and appreciate being taught the appropriate way to treat people in specific situations. It is my challenge to take advantage of every chance I get to help my students become more loving toward one another. Most of the time teenagers aren't completely sure what is right from wrong when it pertains to social etiquette.

I constantly remind students to be slow to anger, and to think before they speak. People love to be called by their "given" names and not their nick names. I typically advise students to say something kind to another student. If they're unable to say something pleasing then I ask them to remain silent. Silence can be golden!

BASIC SCHOOL MANNERS

1. Don't use profanity, as it shows poor upbringing
2. Don't cut off people talking or butt in to tell your story
3. Don't whisper around other people
4. Don't eat or drink in front of other people unless you plan on sharing what you have with them
5. Keep a "hands off" policy to everyone. People hate to be hit, pushed, tantalized, touched, or picked on in any way. It's annoying! Simply keep your hands to yourself!
6. Never be louder than the group you're with. It shows immaturity and how desperate you are for attention.
7. Always speak to everyone to show that you are friendly and kind. It's okay to have "best friends," but don't form "clicks" where you are a snob and exclude others. It is rude at any age not to answer back when someone speaks to you. It only takes one second to say "hello".
8. Always be respectful to your teachers and listen in the classroom.
9. Always smile and talk to your teachers every day.
10. Be sure to do your work to the best of your ability.
11. Never argue with your teacher. If you disagree with something your teacher says or does, schedule a meeting before or after school to talk to them about it in private.
12. Stay seated in the classroom unless you have permission to get up.
13. Never chew food or gum with your mouth open and be sure to leave your lunch table or lunch area spotless.
14. Never talk behind people's back.

Always remember: In order to have a friend, you must be a friend.

Mother, Chita Katherine and I are at a mother-daughter "Chita" reunion in Birmingham, Alabama, July 1992. My daughter is eight years old in this picture. We are at my namesakes daughters house. I wanted Chita Katherine to meet all of the Chitas (that are still alive), so she could understand why I respect our name so much. All of the Chitas are poised, kind and loving women. All of us practiced proper table etiquette at lunch that day and socialized to get to know one another. No one excluded themselves from the reunion in any way. Exclusion in a social setting is rude!

I wanted Chita Katherine to understand her name has family value. It's polite and courteous as a parent to explain to your children the value of their name. I felt like it was my responsibility to explain the significance of her name in the most fun, yet respectful way possible.

There is no doubt that the name Chita is unusual, but it never seemed that way because it was our family name. Simply put, my daughter is named after me. Our family has five generations of mother-daughter Chitas. Three generations are still alive and pictured below:

Sometimes having nice manners just means being kind and loving to others socially.

Even after I was married and had children, Mother would take us to visit our extended family when I flew back to Tennessee for summer vacations. When children grow up visiting with older people they become more compassionate for others.

Katherine Bacon, me, Chita Katherine, and mother

Me, my son Adam, Chita Katherine, and Katherine Bacon

I always took the children to visit extended family when we visited Tennessee. It's the perfect time for a child to practice their social skills with their parent's guidance.

Mother always said to write a personal thank you note to anyone who invites you to their home for a meal or party. You should also write thank you notes to people who entertain you or give you a gift. Special thank you notes should be written to people who honor you with a party. A hand written thank you note is the perfect way to show your appreciation and gratitude. E-mails, texts, and phone calls do not make a person feel as loved and thanked as much as a written card or note mailed to their home address. Personal thank you notes make a person feel loved and appreciated.

Here are three examples of thank you notes that I have received. You can imagine how wonderful they made me feel! Don't forget to write people and thank them for something you appreciate.

Dear Chita,
Thank you so much for hosting yet another party. It was such a beautiful evening. I loved the red carpet. You really went to a lot of trouble to give us such a great night.
I will miss you, but I hope we will get to hang out some time...
Love you,
Debbie

Dear Mrs. Johnson,

Thank you so much for being a great P.E. teacher. You are not just a teacher, you are a teacher that actually cares about us and our health. Thank you for doing so much for Alyssa, Christina, and I we really apperciate it. I hope you love the flowers and I know next year we will have a great time together.

Thanks again,
Sara Bein

Dear Mrs. Johnson,
Thank you so much for teaching me to be a poised young lady and for helping me to improve my presence. I am continuing to go over the 20 poses and also articulating my speech.
I am very excited to put everything I learned into practice and I hope to take another lesson with you in the future! Sincerely, Jarryn P. Murphy

Cell phones sure do come in handy for emergencies, but they should not be answered or used while you are face to face talking to a person. When you are with a friend or a person socially, you should look them in the eye while you talk to them and try not to be distracted by anything else; especially a random call on a cell phone. People love and appreciate your undivided attention when they are talking to you face to face. Mother always said, "Nothing makes me madder or hurts my feelings more than when a person looks away at other things or talks on a phone in front of me when I am talking to them. It's rude!" When you do this to a friend or person you're talking to, it makes them feel unimportant and second best to the person on the phone. It is respectful to stay focused on who you're talking to throughout the entire conversation. This behavior makes a person feel loved and important.

No one likes to hear another person's conversation when they are talking on their cell phone in public. It's simply annoying, distracting and inconsiderate of others. If you take a call and it's an emergency, excuse yourself to a restroom or private area to talk. Don't make calls in front of other people unless it is an emergency.

DATING MANNERS

Boys should go inside the girls' home before each date to visit with the girls' parents before they go out. The guy should discuss his plan for the evening with the girls' parents to see if his ideas are okay. A girl should never meet her date outside the house as long as she is still living at home with her parents. The girl should stand by her car door until her date opens the door for her. The couple should agree to power down their cell phones and all gadgets so they can focus on each other the entire evening. Both people will feel more appreciated and loved that way. The boy should pay for everything unless it's set up otherwise. The boy should have his date home on time (whatever the parents requested). Guys should not kiss the girl on the first date. He should thank her for a wonderful time, and go home. The girl should always thank her date as well. Keep the relationship simple, so there's no drama in case you don't want to date them again.

RESTROOM MANNERS

Whenever you go to the restroom or bathroom at home or away, be sure to flush the toilet and leave the toilet seat down. Always wash your hands thoroughly before you leave the restroom with soap. Try not to be messy in any way by letting paper or water get on the basin, floor, or outside the sink. If you accidentally make a mess, be sure to clean it up before you leave the restroom.

My favorite act of kindness is to reciprocate. I learned as a child to pay people back when they had given something to me through some act of kindness. Mother always said, "They had you over the last time, Chita, now it's your turn to have them to your house." It was important to Mother for me to return hospitality. I learned early on if a friend asked me to lunch and a movie and paid my way to go, then it became my turn to invite them to lunch and movie and I would pay for them. It didn't have to be the exact invitation, but it did have to be something fun and nice so the friend could enjoy themself. It's simply rude when you don't reciprocate. It's not fair when the same people send out the invitations and have to host over and over. Everyone should take turns hosting. I like to reciprocate by having couples to my house for dinner after they have had Paul and I over for dinner. Sometimes we prefer to take them out to a new place we can all enjoy. Whoever does the inviting (written or verbal) is responsible to pay for the bill unless it is set up otherwise. Anytime you are hosting a party in your home or at a restaurant, the hostess should pay the bill.

When friends and relatives come visit you from out of state, remember the next get-together should be you going to stay with them at their house or vacation spot. You should take turns flying back and forth to see each other in order to stay in touch. My mother lives in Tennessee, and every year since 1988 (the year I moved to California), she flies out to see me and visit for a few weeks. I usually fly to Tennessee two or three times a year to visit Mother and the rest of my family. Relationships and friendships are stronger and filled with more love when everyone reciprocates. Just remember: when someone does something nice for you, it becomes your responsibility to do something nice for them.

Whenever anyone talks about something gross or inappropriate at the table or in public don't respond in any way. This allows the conversation to be one sided and the subject usually gets dropped. Treat it just like a dropped call on a cell phone and it will go away. Use the same mannerism when someone embarrasses you or tells a dirty joke.

If one person is dominating the conversation, the hostess should purposefully talk to the people who have talked the least.

Try not to ask people questions when their mouth is full. Timing has a lot to do with having nice manners while talking with people who are eating.

It's best not to talk when you're chewing food. If you are chewing food, and your friend ask you a question, it's okay to hold up one finger in order to indicate it will be one minute until you are ready to talk.

Nice manners and kindness toward others are sometimes a reflection of your up-bringing.

Proper table manners are usually passed down from generation to generation. If your family did not teach you proper table manners, you need to take formal classes in order to educate yourself. You can become more confident in a social situation. Proper manners will relax you and everyone you encounter. People are attracted to people who have nice manners. Many job interviews judge you based on your table manners and social etiquette. No one wants to hire someone who has rude behavior or conversation. They are a poor representation for their company.

I currently offer a two-hour manners/modeling/etiquette class that will guide and instruct you on "dining do's and don'ts", cell phone etiquette, modeling/posture, social introductions, walking and sitting properly, and wardrobe guidelines. The price is negotiable based on class size. Feel free to call me at 909-559-9955 to set up your class date and time. Extensive training is optional.

Hopefully, my life's story and "Mothers Manners" will guide you, encourage you and teach you how to have eloquent manners throughout your life. Thank you!

Printed in the United States
By Bookmasters